About the Author

Emma Lucy Judson was originally born in Leicestershire where she enjoyed a wonderful childhood. Her family would often take her to visit stately homes and castles around Britain which resulted in a real appreciation of British history and the monarchy. Emma has particularly fond memories of visiting London and seeing the changing of the guards. She wanted to write and illustrate a children's book dedicated to Queen Elizabeth II, one which would also provide a lasting reminder of Her Royal Highness for future generations to come.

William of Windsor

Emma Lucy Judson

William of Windsor

Nightingale Books

NIGHTINGALE PAPERBACK

© Copyright 2022
Emma Lucy Judson

A CIP catalogue record for this title is
available from the British Library.
ISBN 978-1-83875-266-8

Nightingale Books is an imprint of
Pegasus Elliot MacKenzie Publishers Ltd.
www.pegasuspublishers.com

First Published in 2022

Nightingale Books
Sheraton House Castle Park
Cambridge England

Printed & Bound in Great Britain

Dedication

This book is dedicated to my mother, Mags and my daughter, Chloe.
The two great loves of my life.

Once upon a time there lived a very ordinary little brown mouse named William.

William lived in a tiny mouse hole at the bottom of a very crooked house, in a very special town called Windsor. The reason that this town was so special to William was because one very important person lived there… Her Majesty The Queen!

Oh, how William loved the queen!

Every day he would sit, waiting patiently in his favourite spot on top of a bright red letter box to see if he could catch a glimpse of the queen riding past in her golden carriage, or maybe sitting at one of the castle windows sipping a cup of steaming hot tea. Every day he would watch in awe as the royal guardsmen marched towards the grand entrance gates and past the throngs of visitors lining up along the streets, all hoping to see the queen.

William knew that the queen was a very special person indeed.

Every night William would return home to his cosy little mouse hole, which he shared with his seven sisters and brothers, and they would run up to him excitedly asking, "Did you see her?"

"What did she look like?"

"Was she wearing her shiny crown?"

"Oh please, William, please say that you saw her!" Each day, William would look downcast, shrug his shoulders, shake his head and say, "Not today."

But William was one determined, ordinary little brown mouse!

Every evening he would lie in bed thinking of cunning ways in which he could try to sneak inside Windsor Castle to see the queen. But there was one thing standing in his way... the formidable royal guardsmen.

Resplendent in their bright scarlet uniforms, with shiny gold buttons, and wearing fantastic black bearskin hats, they guarded the castle day and night. How could an ordinary little brown mouse get past them and enter the castle unnoticed?

"I've got it!" exclaimed William, as he sat, bolt upright in bed. "The hats! The big, fluffy bearskin hats! I can jump from my letter box into one of the guard's hats. They'll never notice me in there!"

That night William had a restless night's sleep full of wild, vivid dreams. Tossing and turning, one minute he dreamt that he was sitting at the queen's table eating dainty cucumber sandwiches on fine, bone china and the next minute he was being chased through the castle by big black bears, rifles at the ready.

It was a risky plan, fraught with danger, but William was one determined, ordinary little brown mouse.

The next morning was a bright and sunny one and William woke, full of nervous excitement. He decided that he would keep his little escapade secret as he did not want to disappoint his little bothers and sisters should his brave plan fail. That morning he climbed up on top of his shiny red letter box, as he did every day, and waited patiently for the royal guards to appear. It was not long before he heard the sound of the regimental band floating up the street and soon he could see a sea of black, bearskin hats on the horizon as the royal guardsmen started their daily march towards him.

The crowds of tourists were cheering, clapping and snap, snap, snapping with their cameras. Suddenly William felt very nervous and butterflies were turning somersaults in his stomach. This was his big moment. Could this ordinary little brown mouse, from a tiny little mouse hole at the bottom of the very crooked house of Windsor, finally get a chance to meet the queen herself? He thought how proud his little brothers and sisters would be if their big brother William came home with such exciting news.

The sound of the trumpets got louder and louder and William's little heart was beating as fast as the drums that accompanied them. The guards were approaching, their big shiny boots stomping in time to the brass band and William was poised nervously, ready to jump.

Under his breath, William quietly muttered, "One… two… threeeee…" and on the count of three, William took a giant leap for all of mousekind. For a few moments everything went black. Head whizzing and heart pounding, William feared the worst. But then he realised, everything felt… soft… and fluffy!

He had made it! He had safely jumped into one of the guard's bearskin hats! He cautiously peered out from inside the tall, fur cap. All around him he could see the visitors whooping and cheering and the other guard's stern faces focused straight ahead towards the castle. He was getting closer! And closer!

This was it! Finally, the moment he had wished for and dreamt of his whole life, he was inside the castle!

With a loud bang, the heavy castle gates closed behind them and the sound echoed around the high, stone walls. Everything went completely silent. Suddenly, there was loud shouting and orders being barked out as the guards took to their positions in the castle grounds. He cautiously looked around him in awe as he saw the inside of the castle, it was so much more beautiful and grander than he could ever have imagined! His dream had come true at last. As the guardsman took his position in his sentry box, William carefully and quietly crawled out of the bearskin hat and hopped onto a small wooden ledge.

How easy it had been to enter the castle grounds! Now where would he find the queen? Being the queen's number one fan, William knew that she tended to prefer to eat her lunches on her own and he thought that would be a perfect opportunity to see her without the fear of one of her guards spotting him in the grand dining room. William quickly made his way through room after room after room – what a huge castle – until he reached the principal dining room.

His poor little heart sank.

There, in front of him, was a danger far worse than the royal guardsmen themselves! Something so ferocious and scary… something worse than he ever could have possibly imagined!

Can you guess what it was? No, not quite fire breathing dragons. It was… THE QUEEN'S CORGIS!

What now? William started to panic, why had he not thought of the queen's favourite dogs! Guardsmen, shiny rifles and big black bears were nothing in comparison with these scary, mouse-catching dogs! Silly William, he absolutely could not fail now that he had made it so far. He puffed out his chest, took a deep breath and then ran for his life, his little legs wobbling underneath him as he nose-dived into a small, metal grate in the floor. Luckily, his tiny little body squeezed through the gap with ease and he was safe.

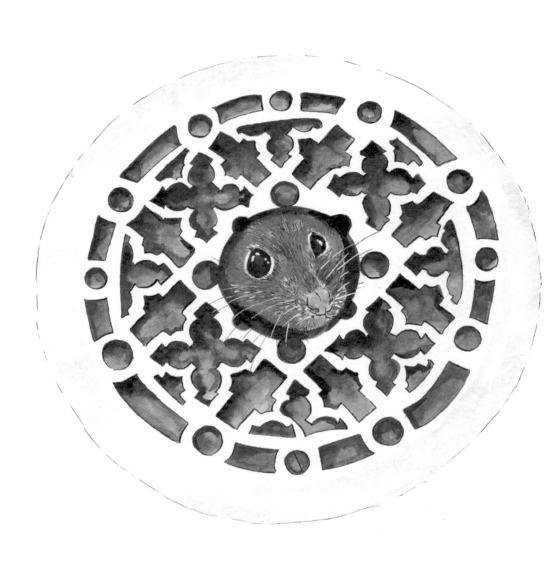

He cautiously peered out, had they spotted him?

"Ahhhh," he sighed, "I think I've managed to escape those savage hounds!" As he looked up to the ceiling his eyes widened to the size of saucers. Above him was the most glorious golden ceiling he had ever seen and in the centre, a glistening chandelier that threw sparkling light all around the room. Grand oil paintings hung on the walls, a log fire roared in the fireplace and sumptuous tables and chairs lined the room. He looked around in wonderment, his bright eyes shining, never had he seen such a beautiful place. Then his heart stopped. He gasped out loud. There she was. There in front of his very own eyes. His very own Queen of England.

Sitting at the grand table he saw Her Majesty tucking into a plate of dainty finger sandwiches, scones and delicious cake. He marvelled at how her shiny crown sparkled under the lights, adorned with glistening diamonds, pearls, sapphires, emeralds and rubies. She was everything he had ever dreamt of and more. Beside her, sitting patiently, were her two corgis – each hoping for even a tiny crumb to fall from her plate. "Oh, you are a greedy boy!" she exclaimed and William watched as she lovingly bent down to pat one of the dogs on his head and then CLONK. William took a sharp breath and looked on in utter disbelief.

Along the table, almost as if in slow motion, rolled one of the bright red rubies from her crown! The queen looked on in horror as her precious jewel then dropped onto the marble floor and kept rolling and rolling.

It was heading straight towards William! He clutched his tail, what was he going to do? His little whiskers quivered. "I must try to save it!" he shouted. Hands outstretched, he watched as the ruby circled around and around the metal grate under which he was hiding and then PLOP! It landed straight into his arms with a thud.

Lying pinned to the floor and holding on to the ruby with dear life, William looked up only to see his very own special queen and her two (still quite scary corgis) looking at him in amazement!

"By jove! I do declare that the little mouse has saved the day! Guards! Help!"

With that, two guards rushed over and the look on their faces was priceless as they saw William pinned underneath the precious jewel apologetically.

"That mouse has saved the day! That little brown mouse deserves a knighthood!" she declared. "Guards, lift up the grate and bring him and my ruby to the dining table immediately!" Dutifully, the guards picked up William and the missing ruby in their big, strong hands and carefully carried him over to the queen.

"What is your name, little mouse?" asked the queen, her face lit up with delight.

Kneeling down in front of the queen he whispered, "William, Your Majesty," his little cheeks blushing.

Taking a small butter knife, the queen gently laid the knife on both his left and then his right shoulder and then she announced, "Arise, Sir William of Windsor. Guards, please fetch Sir William some of our finest cheese for he is to dine with me this afternoon!" The guards swiftly brought William a plump red velvet cushion to sit on, placed a golden napkin around his neck and then offered him a platter of different cheeses from around the world to feast on.

Sir William and Her Majesty The Queen sat together in the grand dining hall, William telling her all about his little brothers and sisters who lived in the tiny mouse hole at the bottom of a very crooked house next to the castle.

The queen made a solemn promise to Sir William that he and his little mouse brothers and sisters, would be welcomed as guests at the castle on this very same day every year. She also promised that a special selection of cheese would be delivered to his tiny little mouse hole every day and that his family would never ever go hungry again.

That night, as he lay awake in his little bed, all snuggled up with his brothers and sisters he thought about that day's adventures. He smiled as he remembered how brave he had been, that coupled with an extra sprinkling of luck and good fortune, confirmed what he had always known, that the queen was a very special person indeed.